THE

OF

YELLOW BEAR

A Pa' Paw Tales Series Chapter Book

Anabeka Inc. Publishing

Published by Anabeka Inc.

The Tale of Yellow Bear
Copyright © 2014 by William T. Holt
Illustrations by Joe M. Ruiz
Cover by Joseph Emnace

Printed in the United States of America

ISBN-10: 0-9885981-2-4
ISBN-13: 978-0-9885981-2-6

Anabeka Inc. Publishing

Questions or Comments? Visit us online at www.PaPawTales.com

Table of Contents

THE TALE

OF

YELLOW BEAR

William T. Holt

PICTURES BY
Joe M. Ruiz

COVER BY
Joseph Emnace

Chapter 1 – Game On

SWEATING LIKE CRAZY WITH HIS HEART POUNDING, Thomas approached the final obstacle of the course. The day was hot, the sun was in his eyes, and it was time to take on the toughest challenge of the race. The impossible Beam Run.

This is no ordinary obstacle, it's a forty-yard dash on an eight inch wide wooden beam suspended six-foot high over a gigantic mud pit and was no easy feat. Thomas has been here before, twice already in previous races, and each time it had been the same result – he had a loss of focus, a loss of balance, a huge splat, and a mouth full of mud!

The toughest part about the final challenge is overcoming exhaustion and all of the distractions. This was his last year at camp and he had to win this time.

Thomas was completely worn out, weakened from dehydration. His arms and hands hurt from scaling the rock wall and the dreaded fifty-foot knotted rope in stage two of the race. His legs trembled from all of the running, squatting, and jumping he had to do, especially across the logger leap challenge he had just completed in stage three. Now, the final challenge standing between him and victory stared him in the face.

Oh yeah, there is one more thing. He was the last one to get there. The other competitors were a few steps onto their beams already and he watched as they were all trying to keep their balance and focus on the thin beams. With arms waiving, and bodies gyrating they struggled just to keep from falling into the mud.

There was a huge crowd cheering loudly, everyone shouting and rooting for their favorite competitor. Thomas took a quick second to compose himself, and to gather his thoughts and attention.

"Come on, you can do this," he said to himself taking in a deep breath. As he exhaled, he scanned through the crowd trying to find the one familiar face that has always provided encouragement no matter what he was going through.

He quickly found it, there standing at the finish line, was his grandfather or as Thomas calls him… "Pa' Paw."

Pa' Paw stared directly at Thomas and made a familiar gesture.

In one swift motion with his hand, he spreads his fingers and covered his face. Then slowly he pulled his hand away making a fist and then the number one with his index finger. This was no ordinary gesture, but a shared reminder between them, a code you could say, one that Thomas understood well. Right away he knew this time would be different.

How you might ask? Well let me tell you the story. It began early one summer morning about six weeks ago…

Chapter 2 – What a Trip

"HAND ME THAT TACKLE BOX, THOMAS," Pa'
Paw said as he flung the camouflage bag containing
the life jackets over his shoulder. It was early morning,
about five thirty… far too early for Thomas. His body
was awake, but his constant yawning was a telltale sign
that his brain and spirit were still under the warm
covers of his bed back at Pa' Paw's house.

On the bright side, he liked fishing and there was
nothing like fresh grilled fish, especially the way Pa'
Paw cooked them. Pa' Paw, however, is what you
would call an early bird. He believed that the best
things in life happen in the peace and stillness of the
dawn, well before the world awakes, bringing with it
the obligations of the day to hijack your thoughts and
demand your time.

They loaded up with all of the gear, both hands filled
with fishing poles, lunch bags, bait, and everything else

needed for a fun day at the lake. It was a bit of a walk to the dock, down a steep hill through a wooded area where one slip could send you tumbling right into the water.

As they headed down to where Pa' Paw's boat was tied, all that could be heard was the peacefulness of the morning and the crackling of the twigs under their feet. As they walked the vaguely familiar path, Thomas readjusted the fishing rods he was carrying and accidentally hit the tree branch above him. Water came cascading down all over them like a quick summer shower.

"Man that was cold!" Thomas exclaimed, arching his back as the icy cold water soaked his shirt and ran down his spine.

"Yeah, it rained pretty good last night," Pa' Paw said in the midst of a giggle. "Watch your step coming down the hill ahead too, it will likely be slippery."

"Don't worry about me," Thomas said confidently as they reached the hill and began their descent. "I am agile like a cat."

As irony would have it, no sooner than the words came out of his mouth, a slick patch of leaves stole his footing and a painful journey to the bottom of the hill began with a thud.

Down the hill he tumbled as the fishing gear went flying in every direction. Thomas covered his head with his hands to keep it from banging up against a big rock or something worse. The sapling trees whipped him all over as gravity increased his speed, hurling him toward the base of the hill and the frigid waters of the lake.

Realizing he had to be close to the water, Thomas tried to grab anything that would help him avoid the inevitable, but it was too late.

Splat! His embarrassing voyage had ended in a big mud puddle that had collected at the base of the hill.

Thomas lay in the mud looking around at the trees towering above him. His head was still spinning as he sat up and put his elbows on his knees, trying to figure out all of his pain spots.

"Man, this really sucks," he muttered to himself as he watched the mixture of mud and blood run down his arm.

He held his shoulder tight, it was really sore. It could have been much worse, he knew, but nothing hurt more than his pride.

"You okay down there?" Thomas heard Pa' Paw call out as he made his way down to the mud pit where Thomas sat.

"Yeah, I'm alright." Thomas answered. He didn't want Pa' Paw to know he was hurt. He had to salvage some of his pride at least.

"I just hate the mud, I mean I really hate the mud," he said as he frantically brushed off the mess of soggy earth, leaves and sticks that littered his body.

Pa' Paw began to chuckle, which made Thomas mad.

"It's not funny!" Thomas shouted as Pa' Paw's giggling continued. He couldn't believe Pa' Paw was making fun of him.

"I could have really been hurt, you know," Thomas said, pushing away Pa' Paw's outstretched hand.

"Well, you aren't hurt which is good, but I do have one question," Pa' Paw said curiously. "When you said you were agile like a cat, just what kind of cat were you imitating? Whatever kind it is, I think it will go through all nine of its lives pretty quickly walking like that!" Pa' Paw could hardly contain his laughter enough to finish the statement.

Thomas wasn't amused, but he began to laugh too, probably more because Pa' Paw was laughing so hard at his own joke that he snorted like a pig, which only made him laugh even harder.

The laughter was a good medicine and it took his mind off the situation for a minute. Pa' Paw had a way of making things light and seeing the bright side of difficult situations. He was cool that way.

Thomas got up out of the mud and began picking up the trail of supplies that had been strewn about during his tumble. After everything was gathered, they got into Pa' Paw's boat and organized their gear to head out.

"Let's go catch the big one," Pa' Paw said as he navigated the boat to the first fishing spot.

Thomas reached down beside the boat and scooped up water with his hand, splashing it in his ear.

"What on earth are you doing?" Pa' Paw asked, totally shocked by his behavior.

"I have to get this stupid mud out of my ear," Thomas said, leaning his head over to let the water drain out.

"What's so bad about a little mud?" Pa' Paw asked.

"I hate the mud, it always reminds me of the obstacle course at camp."

"Why do you play in the mud at camp?"

"I don't play in the mud Pa' Paw, I'm not a baby," Thomas responded, a little offended by the insinuation. "The last obstacle challenge on the course is really tough. I always have problems with it. We have to run across this long beam over a gigantic mud pit and I always seem to fall in, no matter how careful I try to be – it is the worst challenge on the planet!"

Pa' Paw handed Thomas a handkerchief to dry his face as they settled into their spot. He dropped a can full of hardened cement tied to a rope into the water.

"What was that?" Thomas asked.
"That's my anchor," Pa' Paw responded. "It will keep

us floating around when we start catching all of the fish."

They both baited their fishing hooks and made the first casts into the lake. As the bobber settled on the water, Pa' Paw reached over and picked a few bits of mud and twigs out of Thomas's hair and flung them overboard.

"You know, your obstacle challenge reminds me of an old wise tale I once heard when I was your age. If you want to hear it, you may just find a little nugget that will help you through your challenge."

Thomas wasn't really in the mood to talk, but Pa' Paw had the best stories and all he really had to do was listen. Besides, the fish hadn't started biting yet and they needed to do something to pass the time.

"What's the story about?" Thomas asked.

"It's the tale of Yellow Bear," Pa' Paw responded.

"Sure, let's hear it," Thomas said, as he positioned one of the extra life jackets behind his back, and settled in for the story.

"It all happened a long time ago, in a small Indian village," Pa' Paw said as he began telling the tale...

Chapter 3 – The Brave

"THERE ONCE WAS A PEACEFUL TRIBE of Indians who had a good and fair chief named Brave Eagle. The chief had two children - twin sons named Strong Wind and Yellow Bear."

"Were they identical twins?" Thomas asked.

"Yep, identical twins, and they looked exactly alike," Pa' Paw emphasized.

"So how did he tell them apart?" Thomas asked curiously.

"Well, parents can usually tell twins apart pretty easily, but it is interesting you asked," Pa' Paw said, continuing with the story.

"You see, the chief loved his sons dearly and on their first birthday he gave them each a special gift. To Strong Wind he gave a white beaded leather necklace with a dream catcher on it. It was embedded with feathers that blew in the wind.

To Yellow Bear he also gave a necklace, but attached to his was a hand carved, brightly colored, wooden yellow bear.

As time passed, the boys grew strong and they learned many things from their father. They also cherished their father's gifts and wore them all the time. They were so much alike that sometimes the only way to tell them apart was by the necklaces they wore.

Yellow Bear became especially attached to his wooden yellow bear. Once he was asked why he carried it everywhere he went.

"It reminds me of how much my father loves me," he replied.

Now chief Brave Eagle was getting old and knew he soon would have to choose one of his sons to take over as chief. He would watch them carefully to see if one would be outwardly better than the other and often would test them.

"Test them?" Thomas curiously asked. "You mean like the tests I get at school?"

"No – no, these are much tougher challenges." Pa' Paw explained with a chuckle.

"For instance, one day while the chief was walking down by the river, he saw a young mountain lion taking a drink. As he looked at the small size of the mountain lion, he thought to himself, "This would be a great time to test the bravery of one of my sons, a new chief has to be brave." So he went back to the village and found Strong Wind practicing with his bow and arrow. Brave Eagle asked him to go and fetch some water down by the river. Strong Wind put away his bow and arrow, gathered two water buckets and headed toward the river. As he went, the chief quietly followed him in the distance.

"Wait a minute," Thomas interrupted with a tone of concern, "You mean the chief sent his son to the river knowing there was danger there?"

"Sure did, I'm sure he wasn't going to let anything happen to him. That's probably why he followed him," Pa' Paw said.

"When Strong Wind arrived at the river he saw the mountain lion. Out of surprise, he dropped the two water buckets he was carrying. Now he was very afraid because he knew the mountain lion saw him too. The young mountain lion crouched in a stalking position and slowly began approaching him with a hungry look. Although Strong Wind knew he should not look a mountain lion in the eye, in the moment of panic, he couldn't help but stare as it drew closer to him.

So there he was, eyes locked with the young mountain lion and time stood still. He knew he had to make a quick decision whether to run, or to stay and fight. Strong Wind took a deep breath picked up a nearby branch and let out a primal yell. Just then, the mountain lion lunged forward and the battle began. They fought for minutes which seemed like hours.

Brave Eagle watched from the bushes with a nervous anticipation. As much as he wanted to help Strong Wind, he knew he must let him battle alone.

Smack! With a powerful swing of the branch, Strong Wind hit the mountain lion hard under the jaw. The young lion let out a yelp and staggered a bit. Strong Wind didn't waste a moment and he immediately began to hit the mountain lion over and over until the lion, realizing that it would not be able to win the fight, ran off into the forest.

Brave Eagle watched with a father's pride as his son dropped the branch and fell to his knees. Still trembling from the rush of excitement, he gathered his thoughts and inspected his wounds.

Strong Wind collected the water buckets and the water he had come for in the first place. As he headed back he kept a watchful eye for any other animals lurking in the brush.

Brave Eagle hurried back to the village so that he would be there before Strong Wind returned. He was relieved knowing all had ended well and he was proud to know his son was so brave."

Chapter 4 – The Big One

"GRAB YOUR ROD, looks like you are getting a bite!" Pa' Paw exclaimed, as he watched Thomas's fishing bobber bouncing on the water. Thomas picked up his rod and began to slowly turn the crank on the reel to tighten the fishing line. He could feel the fish on the other end nibbling and pulling on the bait. The fishing line began to move in the water, and Thomas got really excited.

"I think he's got it!" Thomas shouted as he snatched back with the rod to try and set the hook. As he pulled back, he felt weight pulling against him. He began to crank the reel faster and faster trying to get the fish to the boat.

"Get the net, I think this is a big one!" he shouted as he began to stand up in the boat. He was pulling back so hard his fishing rod bowed over under the weight of the load.

"Whoa!" Pa' Paw shouted grabbing on to the sides of the boat as it began to rock back and forth from of all the movement.

As the end of the line approached, Thomas could see swirls in different places atop the water. Pa' Paw picked up the net and moved to the edge of the boat where Thomas's fishing line was.

"Get ready Pa' Paw, I'm pulling him out. Man he's heavy." Thomas said as he gave one last big pull.

All of a sudden a stick poked out of the water, then another a few feet away and another until it became disappointingly clear Thomas didn't have a fish at all, but had snagged a branch from under the water and fought it all the way to the boat.

"Ah man, I caught a stupid branch!" Thomas exclaimed in disappointment. He looked over at Pa' Paw who had his head down, clearly trying to hold back the laughter.

"Well... it is a big one," Pa' Paw remarked looking up at Thomas standing in the boat. "Might not taste too good unless you use a lot of lemon," he continued bursting into laughter.

"Ha-ha, very funny," Thomas snapped sarcastically, as he gave Pa' Paw the evil eye and a sneer.

Eventually he smiled... it was funny. Pa' Paw continued to chuckle as he removed the branch from the fishing hook and helped reset the line.

"Now if you want, I can tell you what went wrong there," Pa' Paw offered. "If you do some things a little differently, you might be able to land the next one."

"Sure," Thomas said shyly.

"First things first," Pa' Paw began, "You have to try not to panic. Panicking gets you all worked up. You have to learn to stay in the moment, think about what you need to do and focus on the task at hand."

"I don't get it," Thomas replied, a little confused. "I had to try and hook him before he got away."

"Yes, but you weren't even sure he had the bait before you tried to snatch him out of the water," Pa' Paw clarified. "I will bet your heart was thumping and you could barely think straight, right?"

"Yeah," Thomas said nodding in agreement. "How do you control that?"

"You have to focus, you know, block everything else out. Start with a deep breath to calm your nerves. Then think about the next simplest thing you need to do, then do it," Pa' Paw explained.

"Ok, I think I've got it. Next time can you tell me this to remind me?"

"Well, that's another thing. You were making so much noise you probably scared all the other fish away. You have to be quieter. We have to think of a way to communicate without a lot of talking."

"I guess I was a bit excited," Thomas said, remembering all the yelling he was doing. "Sorry about that."

"No problem little man," Pa' Paw said, handing Thomas another piece of bait for his hook, "Happened to me the first time I went fishing too, except I stood up in the boat and it flipped over. Everything went to the bottom of the lake. Water was so cold, I peed on myself!"

They both laughed as Thomas cast his fishing line back into the water.

"What we need is a code," Pa' Paw said, "Something to remind you to focus all of those wild thoughts into the one thing you need to do."

Pa' Paw thought for a minute.

"Okay, here's what we'll do. I am going to do this," Pa' Paw said as he demonstrated by covering his face with his open hand.

"That means gather your thoughts. Then this motion..." he slowly continued by pulling his hand away from his face and making a fist. "This means you need to focus, take a deep breath and ignore your distractions," he said, giving his fist a little shake. Then he lifted his index finger to make the "number one" sign, saying, "This will mean to focus on the one thing you need to do next. What do you think?"

"Cool! I think I got it. Let's try it next time," Thomas said excitedly.

Pa' Paw checked his line and adjusted his sitting position in the boat.

"So what happened next in the story?" Thomas asked.

"Oh yes, I was telling you a story wasn't I, now where was I?" Pa' Paw said tapping his chin with his fingers.

"Strong Wind just beat the mountain lion," Thomas said quickly settling back into his comfy position.

"That's right," Pa' Paw smiled. "This is where it really gets good."

Thomas listened intently as Pa' Paw continued the tale.

Chapter 5 – Full Bellies

"SO, BACK AT THE VILLAGE people talked of Strong Wind's bravery, especially Yellow Bear, who was his biggest fan. Brave Eagle favored Strong Wind for the position of chief because he had seen his bravery first hand.

A few months went by and it was now hunting season. This was the first time Brave Eagle allowed his sons to be a part of the hunting party. The night before the big hunt, there was a big celebration and a great feast. There was lots of music and dancing around the fires, rituals that helped bring success to the hunt and strength to the hunters. It was extremely important that the hunt was successful, because the meat would feed the entire village throughout the winter.

It was also important that the hunters got plenty to eat and lots of rest for the hunt the following day. Brave Eagle considered the importance of the feast and devised a plan to test the compassion of his sons. A chief should be a brave leader, he reasoned to himself, but he must care for his people and show great compassion too.

So, he sent Yellow Bear and Strong Wind to feed the horses and be sure they were securely tied up in the field. Then he went to one of the ladies in the village who had three small children and told her to keep the children hidden until all of the food was gone."

"First he sends his son to fight a mountain lion, and then he starves some kids? Geez, this guy is mean!" Thomas said interrupting the story.

Pa' Paw chuckled a bit.

"Well, I figure he wanted to make sure the tests were the real deal. Chief is an important position, you know."

"Yeah, I guess," Thomas responded, reaching into the lunch bag and grabbing a ham and cheese sandwich. "All this talk of food is making me hungry."

Pa' Paw smiled and he handed Thomas a bottle of water to drink while he ate the sandwich. Then he continued the tale.

"Now, the feast was ending and there were barely any scraps of food left when the sons returned from their task. There was just enough for them to make a plate for themselves. They sat near the fire where everyone continued to sing and dance. As they began to eat, the children came out to the tables looking for food. Both sons could see they were very hungry."

"Where was the chief during all of this?" Thomas asked.

"Brave Eagle was talking with the elders of the tribe, but kept a close eye on what was happening by the food tables," Pa' Paw said.

"The children soon realized there was nothing left to eat and began to cry. Yellow Bear looked at his food, and although he was very hungry, he knew he couldn't eat in front of hungry children.

He got up and asked one of the women for clean plates. He took the plates over to the children and began to distribute his food to them.

He quickly figured out there would not be enough for all of them. "I have to find more food," he thought to himself, as he finished scraping the last bit of food onto the child's plate. Just then he heard Strong Wind approaching with his food too. They made sure all of the children had enough to eat and went to get some rest.

Brave Eagle watched the entire thing and took note of their compassion. He called over his wife and told her where he had hidden food and for her to take it over to his sons so they could eat.

"How did he know they would give away their food?" Thomas asked.

"He didn't know. I imagine he would have given the hidden food to the children if they did not share."

"Oh, yeah, that makes sense," Thomas said, finishing his sandwich. "I guess he is nicer than I thought."

Pa' Paw gave Thomas a wink and reached into the lunch bag to get a sandwich for himself.

"Seeing you eat made me hungry," Pa' Paw said unwrapping his sandwich.

They both shared a moment of quiet reflection as Pa' Paw ate. Thomas looked around at the stillness of the lake and thought about all of the fun he was having spending time with Pa' Paw and the things he had learned so far.

His clothes were pretty much dry from his mud fall earlier and his shoulder didn't hurt so much anymore. Best of all, it was perfect weather for fishing.

Pa' Paw finished his sandwich and got set to continue with the tale, but as he looked around something caught his attention.

Chapter 6 – Even Again

THOMAS'S FISHING ROD BEGAN TO WIGGLE and move.

"I think you've got another one on the line." Pa' Paw whispered. Thomas reached for his fishing pole nearly knocking it over into the water.

"I am going to catch him this time Pa' Paw!" Thomas shouted as he began to stand up in the boat.

Pa' Paw could see he was getting excited and didn't want him to miss the fish again.

"Psst!" Thomas heard just as he got set to snatch back on the fishing rod.

He gave his attention to Pa' Paw, who didn't say a word. He just covered his face with his open hand. Then slowly he pulled his hand away making a fist and then the number one with his index finger.

Thomas remembered the code right away. He took a deep breath and exhaled as he thought about what he needed to do next.

He watched his bobber as it bounced on the water, but this time he waited until he saw the bobber dip under water and disappear.

Immediately he pulled back on the rod, not too hard this time, just enough to set the hook.

"Gotcha!" Thomas exclaimed as he began to reel the fish in.

He could feel this was a good size fish by the way that it dove deep into the water. He fought it for a few minutes and finally got it near the boat.

Pa' Paw grabbed the long-handled fish net ready to scoop the fish, but there was no need. Thomas reached down, grabbed the fish and pulled it out of the water into the boat. It was no whopper, but it was a good sized fish, plenty to eat for sure.

Thomas removed the hook from the fish's mouth and held it up to show Pa' Paw.

It was a nice largemouth bass, just the right size.

"Not bad for the first fish of the day," Thomas said with a proud smile as he handed the fish to Pa' Paw to put in the fish keeper.

"Yep, not bad at all, great job," Pa' Paw agreed inspecting Thomas's catch.

Just then Pa' Paw got a bite too. Thomas watched carefully as Pa' Paw took his time setting the hook and reeled in his fish. It was another good one. Pa' Paw unhooked the fish and put it in the fish keeper along with the other.

"Thanks Pa' Paw," Thomas said. "The code worked, it really helped me to focus."

"No problem, you did great," Pa' Paw responded. "I am very proud of you."

"Like Brave Eagle was of his sons?" Thomas asked.

"Yes, just like that," Pa' Paw agreed rubbing Thomas's head.

"So what happens next in the story?" Thomas asked.

"Let's get our lines back in the water and I will tell you," Pa' Paw responded.

~~~***~~~

ONCE THEY WERE ALL SET, Pa' Paw continued with the story.

"So it was the day of the big hunt and everyone was set to go. After their morning pre-hunt rituals they headed out before dawn to where the buffalo herds were. When they arrived Brave Eagle laid out the plan.

Part of the hunting group would herd the buffalo toward the other hunters who would take them down with their weapons. Everyone got into position just as daylight began to move across the valley. Yellow Bear and Strong Wind were part of the group herding the buffalo toward the hunters.

Brave Eagle gave the signal and the herders began to yell.

"Eyeee, yieee, yieee, yieee, yah!" Pa' Paw shouted in his best Indian imitation, nearly scaring the daylights out of Thomas.

Thomas sat up with his eyes wide open as he listened to Pa' Paw continue with the tale.

"Buffalo were running everywhere! Yellow Bear, Strong Wind and the other herders were chasing the buffalo towards the other hunters while riding their horses and waving their spears. When the hunters started attacking the buffalo, the buffalo turned back and began running toward the herders.

One of the other young Indian braves named Whistling Moon was on a horse that began to buck wildly. The horse became more and more afraid of the thunderous sound of the stampeding buffalo. One strong buck and Whistling Moon was thrown from his horse.

Crack! He hit the ground hard, breaking his leg. He could see the bone sticking out through the skin. He was in agonizing pain, but now was also helplessly stuck in the path of the oncoming buffalo."

"Ewww, gross!" Thomas said. "His bone was sticking out…ouch!"

Pa' Paw nodded his head in agreement and continued with the tale.

"Yellow Bear saw Whistling Moon on the ground with his broken leg and immediately turned to help him. He arrived just as the charging buffalo reached. He sat up tall on his horse waving his spear wildly at the passing buffalo, which made some of them veer off."

"Where are the other hunters?" Thomas asked anxiously.

"The rest of the hunters didn't see what was going on because they were focused on the rest of the herd, which left Yellow Bear alone to protect his friend." Pa' Paw explained.

"Then, one really huge buffalo came toward Yellow Bear, but it wasn't scared at all, it was angry. It lowered its head, pointing its horns at them and charged. Yellow Bear's frightened horse reared up on its hind legs throwing Yellow Bear to the ground. The horse ran away, as the huge buffalo charged forward.

As the buffalo approached, Yellow Bear dove across Whistling Moon, and grabbed his spear. As he did he landed on a big rock in the ground. He grabbed his shoulder in pain, but had no time to spare. He sat up, anchored the back end of the spear on the rock and raised the spearhead just as the charging buffalo came upon them.

There was a loud thud and a big cloud of dust as the buffalo came crashing down. Brave Eagle looked over and saw the boys in trouble just as the buffalo hit the ground.

"No!" he yelled rushing over to where they were. His heart pounded within his chest as all he could see was dust and blood covering the ground. As he approached the area, he could see a lone moccasin sticking out from under the massive beast. He drew closer expecting to see the worst, but as he looked on the other side of the buffalo, he saw both Yellow Bear and Whistling Moon lying on the ground. They were terrified and exhausted, but okay. The anchored spear had killed the buffalo and made it fall a little to the left, just missing the boys.

Brave Eagle called over some other hunters and they tended to their wounds. The chief hugged Yellow Bear, relieved that he was okay and proud of his bravery. Not only had he saved Whistling Moon's life, but he killed the biggest buffalo of the hunt at the same time.

They worked all day preparing the buffalo to take back to the village. Once they returned the tale of Yellow Bear's bravery quickly spread throughout the village. Everyone called him brave, especially Strong Wind, who was his biggest fan."

"Man that had to be scary," Thomas said, thinking about the story. "What happens now? They are both brave who is the chief going to pick?"

Thomas was really anxious to hear the rest of the story but still wondered how it would help him with his challenge at camp.

"That's where the story gets interesting," Pa' Paw said, as if he could read Thomas's thoughts. "The end of the story is the best part and you might learn a little something to help you at camp. But first, let's head to one more spot before we go. I think the fish are done biting here."

They reeled in their lines and pulled up the anchor. Pa' Paw started the motor and they headed to another one of his favorite spots. As they rode along in the boat, Thomas thought of all the different ways the story could end. At last, they reached the fishing spot and anchored the boat. He could hardly wait to hear what happened next.

Chapter 7 – Straight Line Decision

"AS WINTER SET IN, Brave Eagle became very ill and knew he would have to pick his successor soon. He struggled with the decision because he was proud of both his sons and they were truly equal in so many ways. He thought hard about his dilemma and decided to consult with the elders.

He called the elders together for a meeting and explained his challenge. They all agreed that it was a tough decision and began giving Brave Eagle many good suggestions of how to make his decision. They also prayed to Great Spirit to give him wisdom to decide.

After the meeting ended, he was still not quite sure what to do. It had begun to snow as he walked back to his dwelling, deep in thought. Time was growing short and the decision had to be made.

That night, Brave Eagle had a dream. In his dream he could see one of his sons running straight toward him with an intense focused stare. Running behind him was every man, woman, boy, and girl of the tribe. He couldn't see which son was running toward him, but he knew this was his choice and they would be able to lead his people with courage, heart, and great vision for the future. Immediately Brave Eagle awoke, he knew just how he would make his decision.

It was early in the morning, just before dawn. He bundled up and went out to get his sons. As they walked with their father in the crisp cold silence, they wondered what this was all about. The snow continued to fall heavily, covering everything in a soft white blanket. As they walked, the only sound you could hear was their footsteps crunching the snow beneath their feet as they walked along a familiar path.

Brave Eagle took them out to a huge open field lined with bare trees. It was the place where they trained for the hunt and played skill games with the other braves of the village. As they entered the field, Brave Eagle stopped and turned towards his sons, his weathered face full of concern.

"My sons, my time is near," he said to them, "Today I will choose the new chief, and my decision is a hard one because you both make me very proud. Still, I can only choose one of you."

Both of his sons understood and promised that whomever he did not choose would help the other take care of the people. Happy to see that his sons were so willing to cooperate with each other, Brave Eagle walked a few steps further into the field and again turned towards his sons.

Pointing to his footsteps he said, "This field is covered with fresh snow so when you walk the path is able to be seen.

I will walk around to the far side of the field and I want each of you to run to me. The one who runs the straightest line will become the new chief."

Both sons looked at each other a little confused. "The snow is falling heavily. What will a straight line show you father?" Strong Wind asked.

"To run a straight line, one must keep your eye on your goal," answered Brave Eagle, "and a good chief must be able to keep focused on his goal and what is best for his people, no matter what is going on around him. Do you have any other questions before we begin?" he asked.

Yellow Bear thought for a moment and then he removed his necklace with the brightly colored hand-carved wooden yellow bear on it.

"Would you hold this for me please?" Yellow Bear asked, as he placed the necklace around his father's neck.

Brave Eagle agreed and then walked around the field to the other side.

"I will go first," said Strong Wind confidently. "I am a very focused person, I am sure that my line will be as straight as an arrow."

Both sons looked far across the field towards their father. But with the dim light of the morning and the distraction of the falling snow, they could barely see him standing on the other side of the field.

Once he saw his father raise his hand, Strong Wind began to jog very slowly. He watched his feet carefully making sure one foot went directly in front of the other. As he started to run, he began to look back to see if his line was straight, each time he did, he made a bad step and had to correct it. By the time he reached his father, his path through the field was not as straight as he thought.

"How is that father?" Strong Wind asked.

Brave Eagle turned him around so that he could see the zigzags he had made.

"It is hard to see where you are going when you are looking behind you, my son," he said.

Brave Eagle then raised his hand for Yellow Bear to begin. Before Yellow Bear started to run he looked across the field, although he could not see his father very well, he could clearly see the bright yellow wooden bear hanging from the necklace around his father's neck.

He focused on the wooden yellow bear and began to run. He ran slowly at first, and then a little faster, then faster, and faster, never once looking away from the yellow bear.

As he ran and continued to concentrate on the little yellow bear, he thought more, and more of how much his father loved him, this made him run even faster toward that love.

When he reached his father, he was running so fast the chief had to catch him in his arms. Brave Eagle smiled at Yellow Bear and turned him around to see his path which was as straight as an arrow.

"Well done son, you kept your eyes on your goal, and your path proves it. You will be the new chief."

When they returned to the village, Brave Eagle called everyone together and announced the news. Everyone cheered for Yellow Bear and they prepared a feast in his honor. Once Yellow Bear became chief, with help from his brother, he led the people as bravely, fairly and kindly as his father and they continued to live in peace and happiness. The End." Pa' Paw said.

"Wow, that was a great story," Thomas said. "You are right, I think I know just what to do the next time I face the obstacle course challenge."

They finished the day after catching a few more fish and had a great time. After they docked and unloaded the boat, they headed home. As they headed back, Thomas thought about the tale of Yellow Bear and all he had learned. It was now time to put all of this new knowledge in to action at the obstacle course.

Chapter 8 – The Great Finish

THOMAS SNAPPED OUT OF HIS DAY DREAM
and realized he was now behind and the last one to
reach the Beam Run Challenge. Pa' Paw walked to the
end of the beam Thomas was on and stared directly at
him, and again, made the now familiar gesture. In one
swift motion he spread his fingers and covered his
face. Then slowly, he pulled his hand away, making a
fist, and then the number one with his index finger.

Thomas took another deep breath to calm his nerves
and then stepped up onto the beam. He glanced
around at the other competitors as they struggled to
stay out of the mud pit below. He looked past the far
end of the beam at the finish line where Pa' Paw was
standing.

"Focus, just like Yellow Bear." Thomas muttered to himself.

Through the cheering crowd he began to focus on Pa' Paw.

He thought about how much he wanted to make Pa' Paw proud.

He thought about the day at the lake and in his mind he could hear Pa' Paw saying "Just focus on the one thing you need to do next, then do it."

The more attention he directed towards Pa' Paw, the less noise and distraction he heard around him. Until it was like they were the only ones there.

He started to take a few steps on the beam, but this time he didn't look at his feet, nor the people around him or the mud below, he just focused on Pa' Paw. Each step he took, he could feel the solid footing on the beam, which gave him more confidence and he began to jog.

He quickly caught up to the other competitors who had started before him, but Thomas didn't realize it because all of his attention was focused on Pa' Paw and on his goal.

He continued to gain speed and was now running on the beam, passing all of the others as they fought to keep their balance. With each solid stride, his self-assurance grew and fueled his motivation. He no longer felt tired or sore, just the intense desire to get to Pa' Paw and finish the race.

The crowd began to cheer louder and louder as he ran faster and faster down the beam toward the end. Thomas began to listen to the cheers of the crowd, he realized he was winning and for a brief moment – he lost focus. As he reached the end of the beam, his foot slipped and he stumbled. His arms waved wildly as he tried to keep his balance.

Only the front part of his foot caught the beam on his next step, but it wasn't enough to hold his weight and he fell from the beam. He reached for anything to grab as he dropped to the ground, but nothing was close and he hit the ground hard.

Like a huge sound wave, the intense volume of the cheering crowd came flooding in. His head was spinning, but he didn't feel any major pain.

"Oooooo!" Everyone gasped loudly at once.

Thomas was still a little dizzy from the fall as he picked himself up from the ground. Suddenly he realized he hit the ground, not the mud. He made it! He couldn't believe he finally made it across the Beam Run without falling into the mud.

The moment of joy was quickly dashed by the sound of another competitor jumping down off his beam. The race wasn't over and he had to get moving. Thomas started running again and heard more people coming off their beams racing to the finish line. He refocused his attention on Pa' Paw and ran with all of his might. Thomas knew that the race was tight and as much as he wanted to look and see where the other competitors were, he kept his eyes on Pa' Paw and the finish.

"You can do it! Focus!" Pa' Paw shouted.

Thomas knew he had to push hard to win the race, so he ran as fast as his legs would go.

He lunged forward as he ran through the finish line right into the arms of Pa' Paw.

His heart was pounding and he was completely worn out.

"I did it Pa' Paw, I did it!" Thomas said, as he struggled to catch his breath.

"You sure did!" Pa' Paw said as he hugged him. "I am so proud of you."

Thomas held tight to Pa' Paw, not only because he was exhausted, or because he was happy that he won. It was because he knew he had learned to overcome his greatest challenge, and with that, he could do anything.

After catching his breath and a few cups of water to quench his thirst, Thomas was called up to the podium and announced as the winner. He held his trophy high in the air and listened proudly as everyone cheered.

It was a great day, maybe he wasn't a new Indian Chief, but like Yellow Bear he was able to focus on his goal and become a winner.

The End.

About the Author

Passionate about making a difference, William T. Holt strives to inspire readers to be creative, learn everyday and have fun in all you do! Whether mentoring through organizations or with his own four children at home, his focus and reward has always been to positively impact the lives of others.

When William is not writing or otherwise working hard, this father of four enjoys sports, arts, and spending time with his wife and family in the South Florida sunshine.

About the Illustrator

Joe M. Ruiz: Born in Florence, Arizona, and studied art at Santa Barbara Community College and the San Francisco Art Institute. Joe has been making art of one kind or another professionally for over 25 years. He lives in Georgia with his wife, 2 kids, one cat, a dog and six chickens.

About the Pa' Paw Tales

The Pa' Paw Tales is a series of children's books dedicated to teaching "old school" core values to a new generation of children - with the creativity and heart of yesteryear. Each story, based on true events, shows the fun of learning while teaching the wisdom of life's greatest lessons. Based on the true events in the life of the author William T. Holt where youthful summers spent with his "Pa' Paw" in the North Carolina countryside, gave birth to these fun tales of adventure and character.

These creative stories aim to not only entertain, but encourage literacy, build core character values and promote the bond of mentoring friendships for all ages.

Pa' Paw
TALES

Made in the USA
Columbia, SC
05 August 2024

39342443R30039